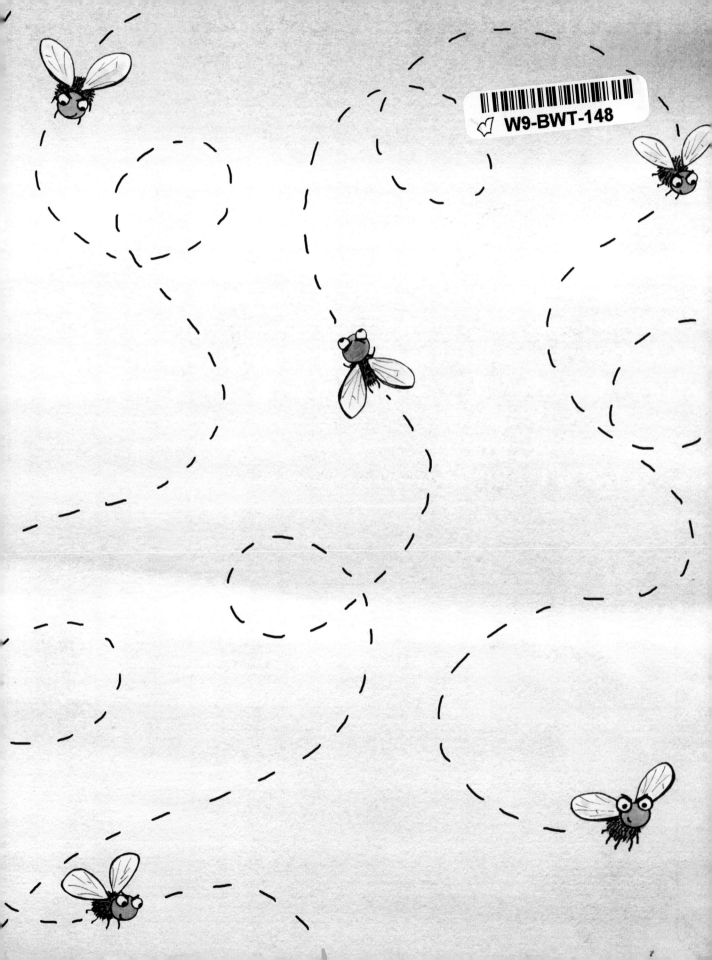

Bye Bye Pesky Fly

by Lysa Mullady

illustrated by Janet McDonnell

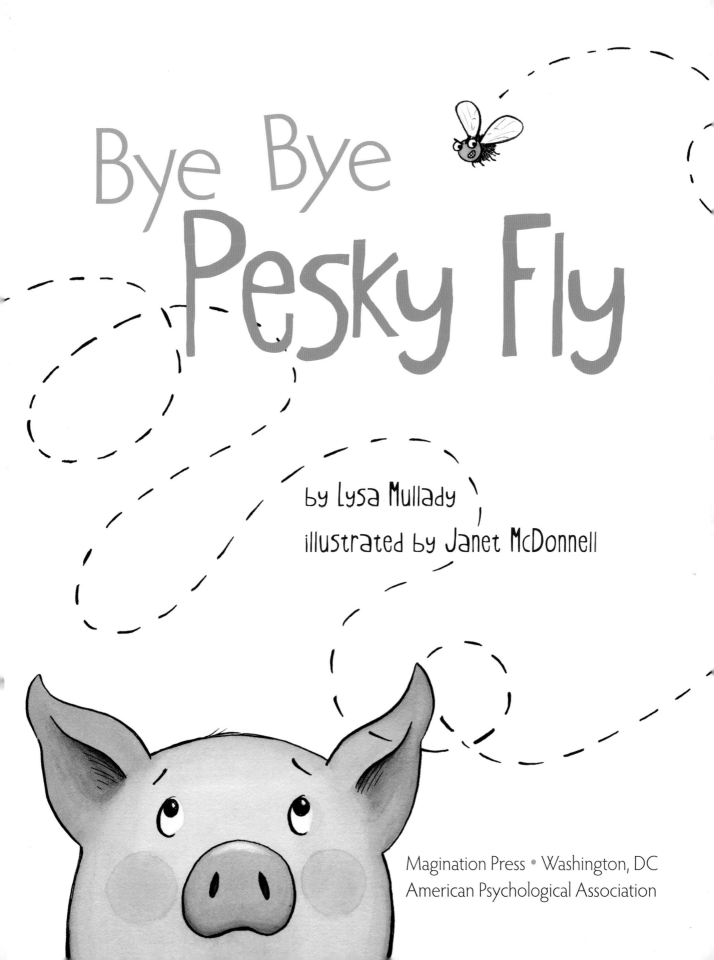

Magination Press • Washington, DC
American Psychological Association

For Derik; thank you for the inspiration–LM

For Sam and Owen, whose sunny thoughts
make them very good company indeed–JM

Published by
MAGINATION PRESS ®
American Psychological Association
750 First Street NE
Washington, DC 20002

Magination Press is a registered trademark of the American Psychological Association.

For more information about our books, including a complete catalog, please write to us, call 1-800-374-2721, or visit our website at www.apa.org/pubs/magination.

Book design by Sandra Kimbell
Printed by Lake Book Manufacturing, Inc., Melrose Park, IL

Library of Congress Cataloging-in-Publication Data

Names: Mullady, Lysa, author. | McDonnell, Janet, 1962- illustrator.
Title: Bye bye pesky fly / by Lysa Mullady ; illustrated by Janet McDonnell.
Description: Washington, DC : Magination Press, [2018]
Identifiers: LCCN 2017032762| ISBN 9781433828553 (hardcover) | ISBN 1433828553 (hardcover)
Subjects: LCSH: Interpersonal relations in children—Juvenile literature. | Interpersonal conflict in children—Juvenile literature.
Classification: LCC BF723.I646 M85 2018 | DDC 155.4/192—dc23 LC record available at https://lccn.loc.gov/2017032762

Manufactured in the United States of America
10 9 8 7 6 5 4 3 2 1

Some days are good days.
Calm, peaceful, and happy.

Pig was having a feel-good kind of day. Pig was just hanging around, thinking about his favorite things. Sunshine, rainbows, and the feel of cool mud on a hot summer day.

Then out of the blue came a Pesky Fly.

That Pesky Fly buzzed around Pig's nose.

That Pesky Fly buzzed around Pig's ears.

Before he knew it, Pig was feeling bothered by all that buzzing. Pig stopped thinking about sunshine, rainbows, and the feel of cool mud on a hot summer day. Now he was thinking about rain, thunder, and prickly sticker bushes.

Pig felt angry and mad. He really wanted to have a happy day.
Would Pig let that Pesky Fly take away his happy day?
No!

What should Pig do?
He imagined yelling at that Pesky Fly.

No.
Yelling makes a problem bigger.

Pig could run away and hide in a cave.

No.

Running away doesn't help. He would still feel upset.
And lonely too.

Could he swat that Pesky Fly?

Never.

Pig was a pig of peace.

He knew it was wrong to hurt anyone or anything.

Pig had to do something about his feelings to feel better. He needed to shake out the itchy feeling he gets under his skin when his mood turns sour. Pig decided that he wanted to feel calm, peaceful, and happy.

He took a deep breath.
He thought about sunshine, rainbows, and the feel of cool mud on a hot summer day.

Pig decided to walk.
Pig whistled a happy tune.
That Pesky Fly flew along.

That Pesky Fly buzzed around Pig's ears.

That Pesky Fly buzzed around Pig's nose,
then landed looking Pig right in the eyes.

Pig remained calm and nicely said,
"Fly, I feel bothered when you buzz near my ears and nose.
Please don't fly so close."

That Pesky Fly flew off Pig's nose, putting some space between them.

"Thank you," said Pig.

That Pesky Fly realized that he had indeed been a pesky fly.

Now, that Pesky Fly had to decide what to do.
He imagined yelling at Pig.

No.
That wouldn't be nice.
Pig had the right to feel his own feelings.

He could fly away and be pesky to someone else.

No.

That wouldn't be nice either.

That Pesky Fly decided Pig was good company.
That Pesky Fly enjoyed sharing the sunshine.

That Pesky Fly liked the cheerful tune Pig whistled while he walked. That Pesky Fly decided a friend was a good thing to have.

"Sorry, Pig. I promise not to buzz too close.
Mind if I tag along?"
"Not at all," replied Pig.

That Pesky Fly was true to his word.
That Pesky Fly flew by Pig's side.

Together they shared the sunshine, rainbows,
and the feel-good kind of day.
That Pesky Fly wasn't pesky any more.

Bye bye, Pesky Fly.

Hello, Friend!

Notes to Parents, Caregivers, and Professionals

Frustration happens every day. Kids are often quick to blame others for causing them irritation, focusing on the cause of their annoyance instead of on how to deal with it. Frustration tolerance is a social skill that leads to positive interactions with both peers and adults. We need to help kids understand the power of remaining calm when something or someone is annoying. After all, we can't stop frustrating things from happening, but we can control how we react.

How This Book Can Help

The story of Pig and Fly walks children through the experience of being annoyed and the choices they can make to deal with it. It illustrates consequences, the benefits of remaining calm, and how to act in an assertive manner. In the story, we see examples of aggressive, passive, and assertive behaviors. Aggressive behaviors (like Pig's thought of swatting Fly!) hurt others and always make the problem bigger. Being passive (like running away) does nothing to solve the problem, so the problem will never go away. Being assertive means you are taking positive steps to handle your problem. Pig regains his peaceful feelings once he acts in a calm and assertive way.

Friendship is so important to children, but can be a fragile thing, especially for kids who are still learning proper social conventions. In the end, both Pig and Fly choose positive actions and are rewarded with the pleasure of each other's company.

The story shifts perspectives from Pig to Fly in order to help kids develop compassion. It's easy to think Fly was being annoying on purpose, but you truly never know why anyone acts the way they do. It turns out Pesky Fly didn't want to be Pesky at all. Ultimately, Fly just wanted a friend. Fly needed to look at how his behavior affected Pig.

Helping Children Deal With Frustration

Pig thinks through his choices. When frustration strikes, it is important to stop and think about how to handle the problem.

Identify feelings. Pig starts the story enjoying his ideal, happy day. We all have our own experiences that make us feel good inside. In order to teach children frustration tolerance, they first need to know what it is like to feel peaceful. As a parent, you can teach this by commenting on how good you feel when you are sharing a moment of harmony with your child. You can reinforce this understanding by asking your child to tell you the things that make them feel good inside. Help them make a list of their feel-good things and keep it in a special place. Take time each day to share and reflect on happy thoughts. This is the first step in being ready to face whatever comes our way!

Model coping skills. Once we recognize a shift in our feelings, we need to decide what to do about it. You can help your child recognize this moment by sharing events that happen to you that threaten to take away your peace. These can be simple things: the newspaper arriving late, litter on the street, getting caught in the rain, a grumpy sales person. Remark how you felt annoyed, but decided it is more important to stay calm. Don't blame the irritant for your feelings; focus on your choice to stay at peace. Kids need to understand that it is not our job to change the situation, it is our job to cope with the result. When you see your child experiencing frustration, coach them through accepting the fact that feeling annoyed happens to everyone, and discuss productive ways they could handle the problem.

Get moving. In his quest to feel peaceful, Pig illustrates how physical activity directly impacts your emotions. Frustration can arrive with such intensity, sometimes it is hard to think clearly. Deep breathing and movement help, and are sometimes necessary, to cool down in order to regain your composure. Pig takes a deep breath, walks, and whistles a happy tune. All of these are examples of calming techniques. There are lots of ways to help your child cool down: Count to ten, squeeze a ball, push-ups against the wall, getting a drink of water, etc. The best thing you as a caregiver can do is to use a calm and reassuring voice until their wave of negative emotion passes. And don't just use calming techniques when your child is feeling frustrated—practice every day! Kids love to move. Have fun with your child! Stretch and reach for the stars, put on music and have a dance party, skip to the car, race in the park. These things are guaranteed to make both of you laugh and smile. After, remark how great it feels to move your body, and emphasize how they could use these actions to feel better when they're not having such a feel-good kind of day. If kids are prepared with these tools ahead of time, it's much easier for them to self-regulate when negative emotions do come along.

Practice talking it out. Pig uses his words to help the situation, but talking it out is easier said than done! Model and practice this skill often with children. Use the script, "I felt ____ when ____." This will illustrate the difference between a feeling and an action. Depending on their age, kids can have trouble telling them apart. Teach them the difference, but also how they affect each other. We all want to get along with others. When someone does something that bothers you, it's only fair to let them know what they did to make you feel upset. Kids are quick to use words filled with blame. Emphasize that if you use hurtful words when talking it out, that is the same as being aggressive and you will make the problem worse.

This story has a happy ending. That's not always the case in real life. If the situation is more serious— if it progresses to bullying or inappropriate behavior— or is persistent, it's important for the child to seek the help of a responsible adult. Pig was able to solve the problem on his own. In cases of being annoyed by another person's actions, kids can use their own conflict resolution skills. When you see your child making good problem solving choices, praise them. Tell them how proud you are that they can take care of their own feelings. We are in charge of the things we think, feel, and do. You can't make someone be nice to you, but you can choose to do the right thing so you can feel peaceful inside. Kids understand the idea of what goes around, comes around. Remind them to be patient. Good things come to those who do good things. When you choose to be friendly, true friends will surely come your way.

About the Author

Lysa Mullady has been an elementary school counselor for 28 years. She is known for her engaging, enthusiastic, and creative counseling style. Her passion is to teach her students to be problem solvers by talking it out and thinking good things. Lysa was born and raised on Long Island, where she still lives with her family and two golden-doodles. You can find her on the weekends enjoying the beach with her husband, walking the dogs and searching for beach glass, all while imagining ways to help others become the best they can be.

About the Illustrator

Janet McDonnell is an illustrator and author living in the calm outskirts of the windy city with her husband and two sons, where she loves drawing peaceful pigs and friendly flies. In addition to illustrating books, magazines, and puzzles, Janet has both taught and written for children from preschool to high school ages.

About Magination Press

Magination Press is an imprint of the American Psychological Association, the largest scientific and professional organization representing psychologists in the United States and the largest association of psychologists worldwide.

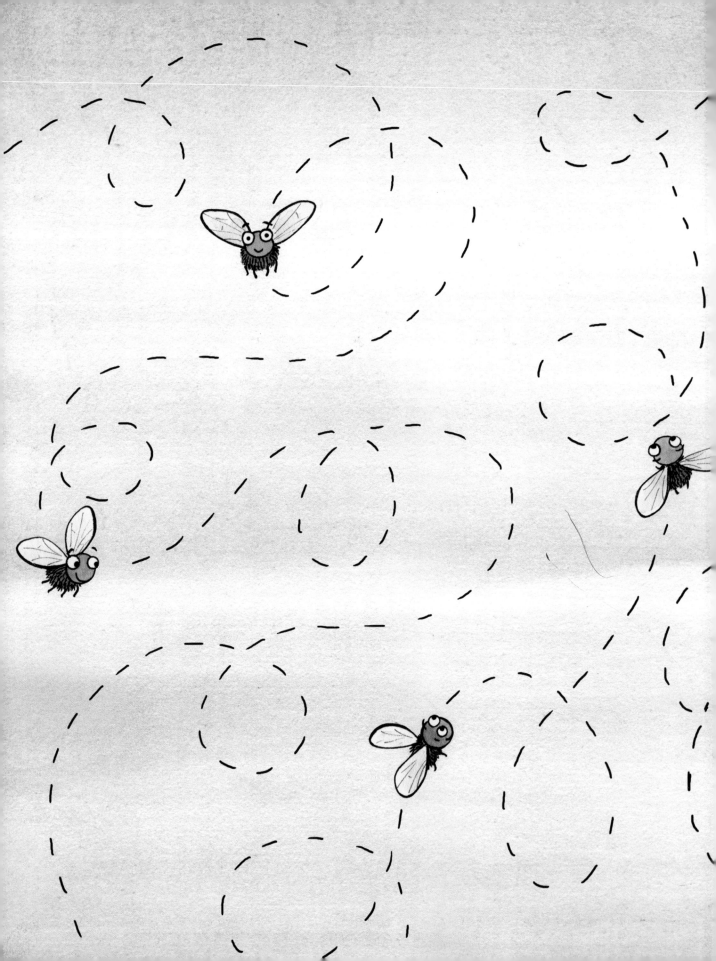